~~Mother Goose~~ Bruce

RYAN T. HIGGINS

Disney • HYPERION
Los Angeles   New York

For Griffin, the silliest goose I know

Thanks to my editor, Rotem Moscovich,
and designer, Whitney Manger,
for their help in cooking up this book.

Copyright © 2015 by Ryan T. Higgins

First Edition, November 2015 · 10 9 8 7 6 5 4 3 2 1 · H106-9333-5-15288 · Printed in Malaysia

Library of Congress Cataloging-in-Publication Data
Higgins, Ryan T., author, illustrator.
Mother Bruce / by Ryan T. Higgins.—First edition.
pages cm
Summary: Bruce is a grumpy bear who likes no one and nothing but cooked eggs,
but when some eggs he was planning to boil hatch and the goslings believe
he is their mother, he must try to make the best of the situation.
ISBN 978-1-4847-3088-1—ISBN 1-4847-3088-7
[1. Bears—Fiction. 2. Geese—Fiction. 3. Animals—Infancy—Fiction. 4. Eggs—Fiction.] I. Title.
PZ7.H534962Mot 2015
[E]—dc23
2014045992

Reinforced binding

Visit www.DisneyBooks.com

He was
a grump.

Bruce was a
bear who
lived all by
himself.

He did NOT
like sunny days.

He did NOT like rain.

He did NOT like cute little animals.

But Bruce didn't eat eggs raw like other bears.

Instead, he cooked them into fancy recipes that he found on the internet.

One day, Bruce came across a recipe for hard-boiled goose eggs drizzled with honey-salmon sauce.

So he went out to get the ingredients.

Last, he went to Mrs. Goose's nest to pay her a visit.

Are these eggs free-range organic?

Then he collected honey from a local beehive.

He liked to support local business, you see.

First, he caught a few salmon.

At home, Bruce prepared the eggs for hard-boiling.

But the fire in his stove fizzled. So he went out to get more wood.

When Bruce came back, he was met with an unwelcome surprise.

Bruce became the victim of mistaken identity.

Bruce wanted
hard-boiled eggs,
NOT goslings.

He supposed he could settle
for buttered goslings on toast . . . .

but for some reason, he lost his appetite.

Bruce scooped up the little geese and stomped back to their nest . . .

only to find Mrs. Goose had flown south early.

Bruce left the goslings there anyway and went back home.

But he was followed.

Bruce was very stern and said things like

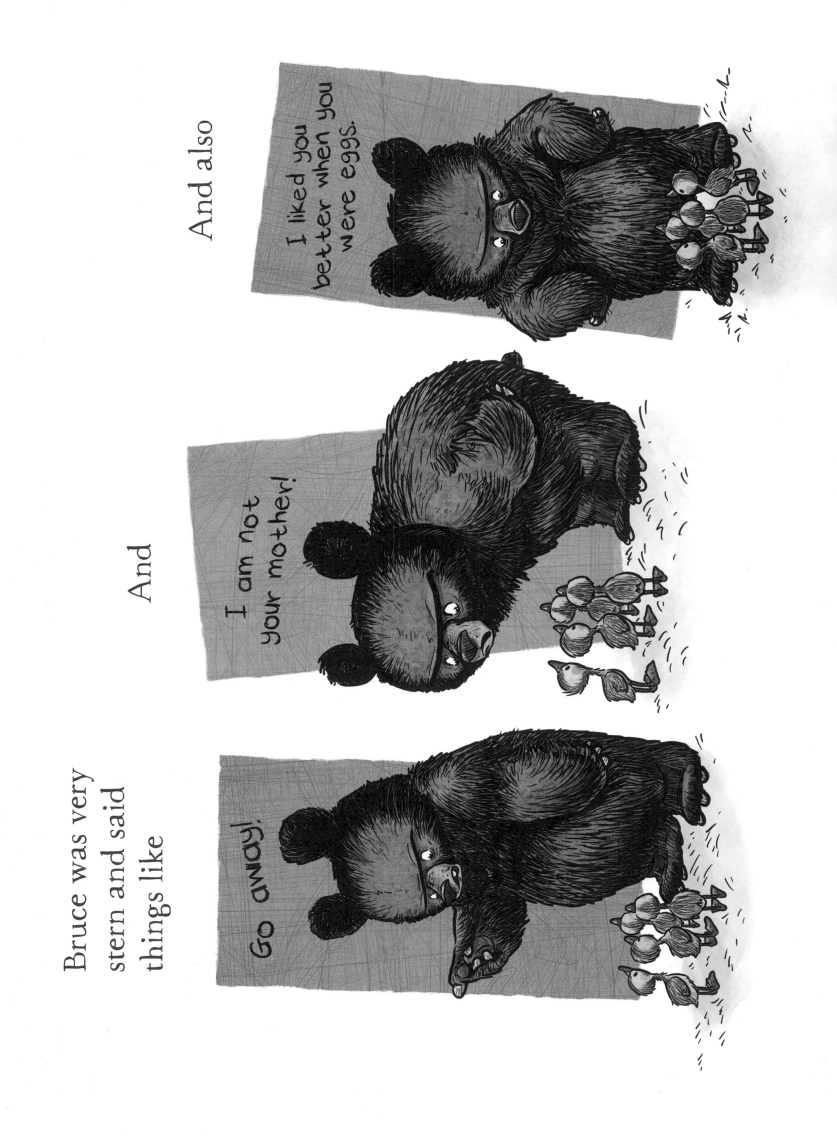

Go away!

And

I am not your mother!

And also

I liked you better when you were eggs.

Bruce could take it no longer and became EXTRA grumpy with them.

It didn't work.

Goslings always
follow their mother,
even if SHE
is a HE and
HE is a bear.

Mama?

Mama?

Bruce was stuck with them.

He tried to make the best of it.

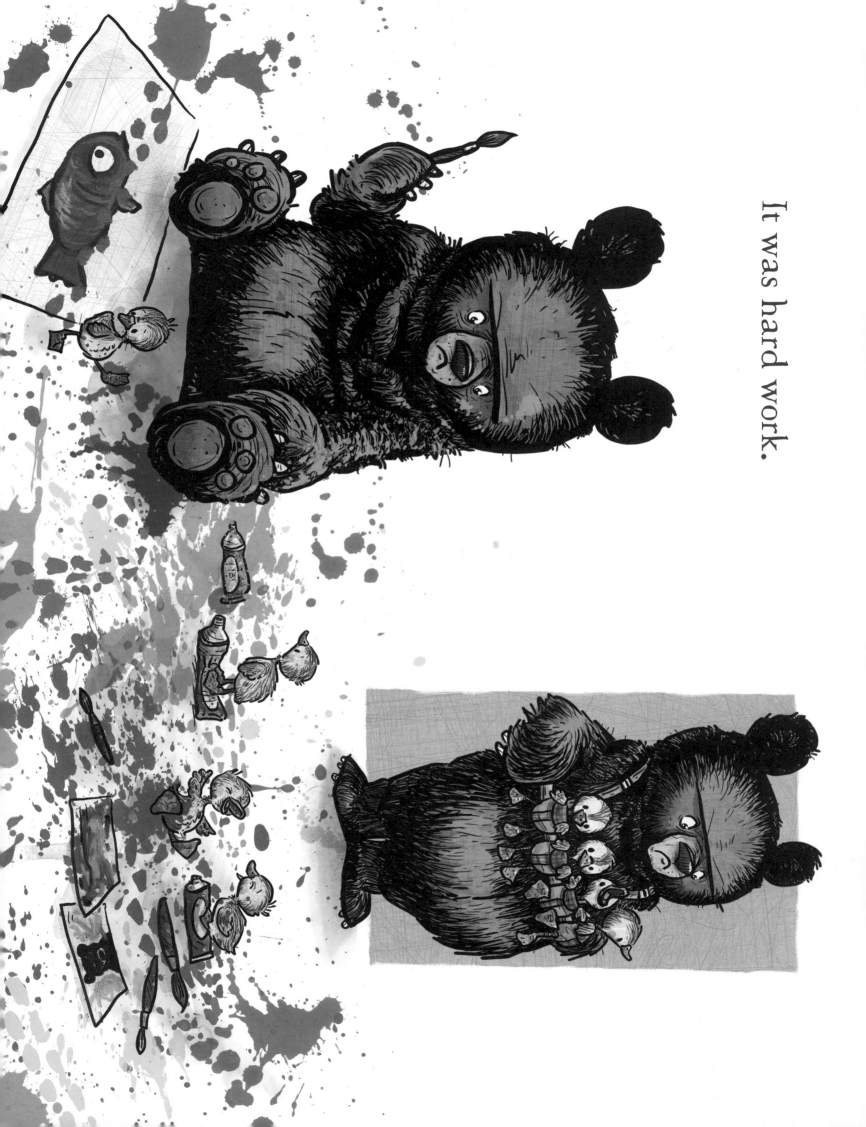

It was hard work.

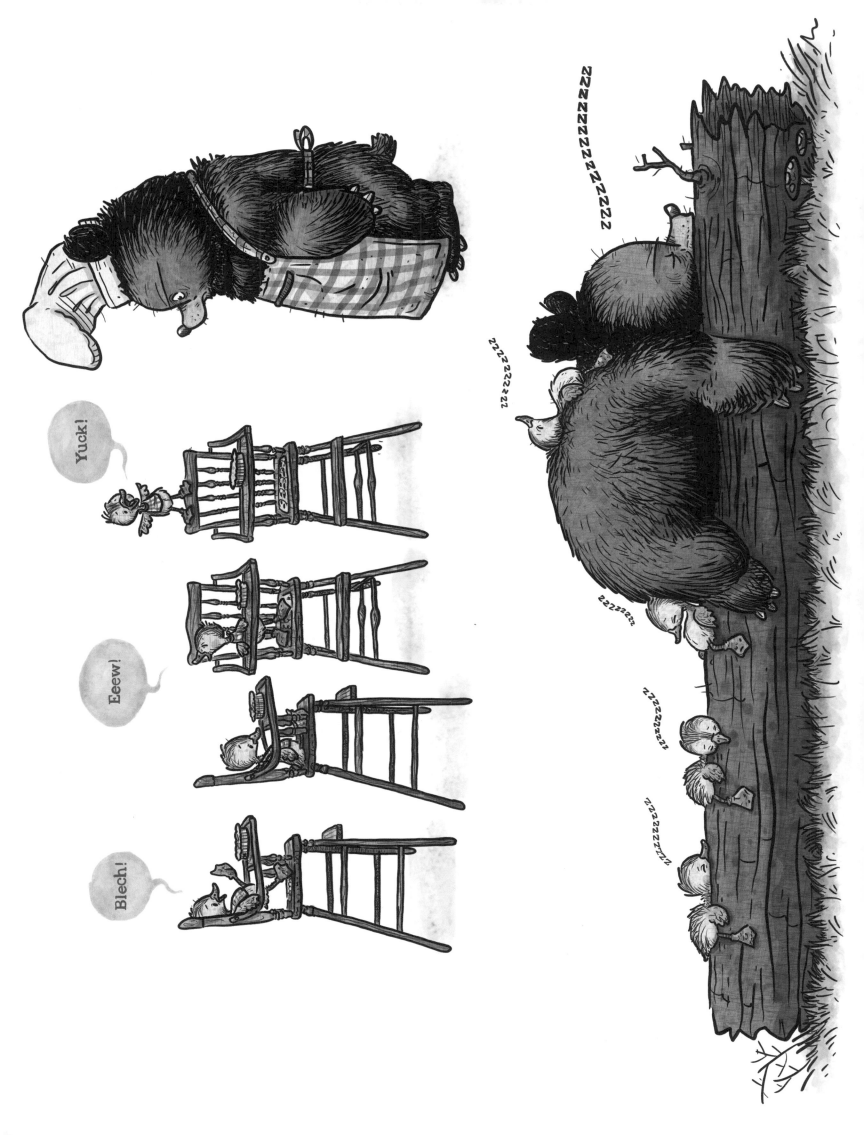

As the seasons passed,
Bruce watched
the pesky goslings
grow older.

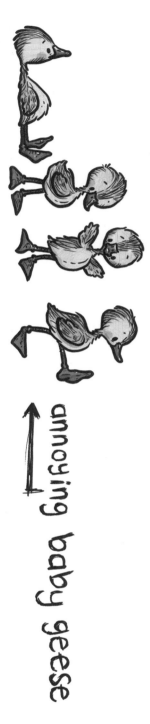

annoying baby geese

Stubborn
teenage
geese

boring adult geese

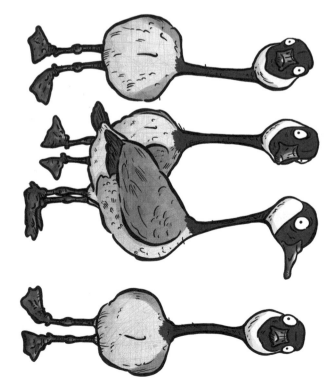

Then one fall afternoon,
he saw other goose families flying south.

Finally, he'd be rid of those geese,
and he could take a long winter nap.

Bruce explained migration.

But they didn't listen.

Bruce needed the geese to leave.
So he got creative.

Nothing worked.

The geese would not leave Bruce.

Sigh . . . .

So Bruce decided to pack some bags and take his geese into town.

They boarded a bus . . .

. . . and migrated to Miami.

Now every winter,
Bruce and his geese
head south together.

They laze about at the beach
in tacky shirts, sipping ice-cold
lemonade, while Bruce dreams
of new recipes —
recipes that don't hatch!

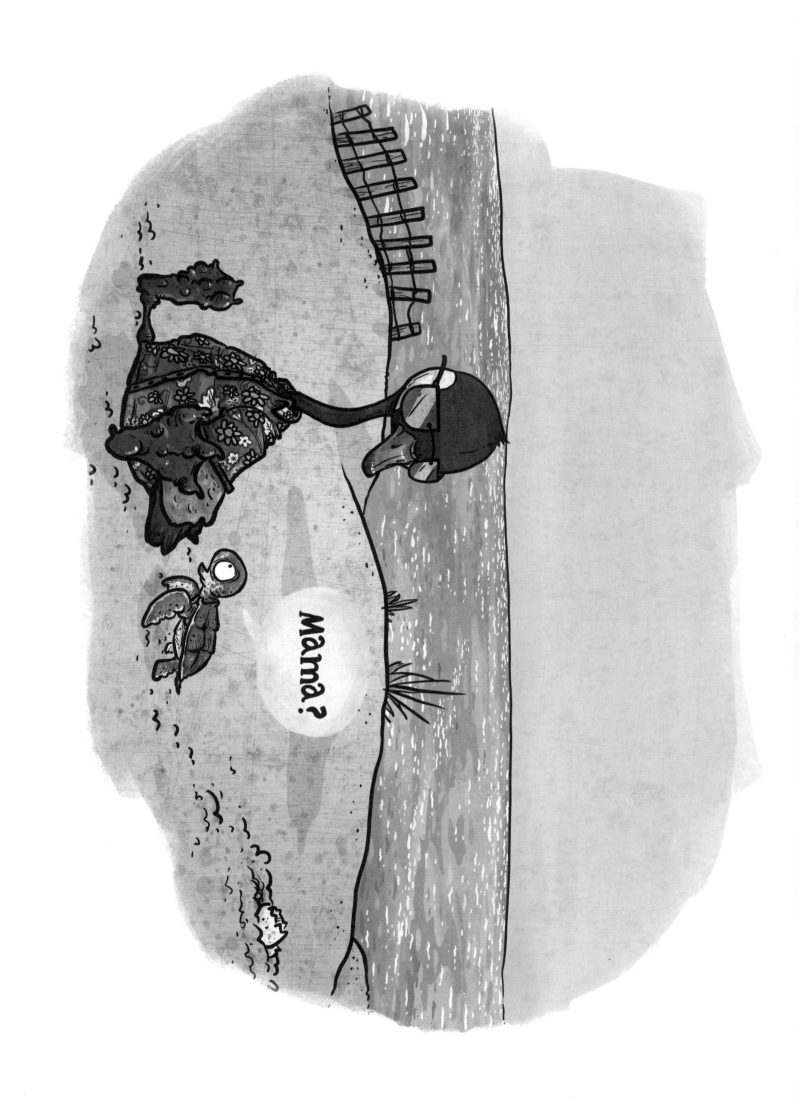

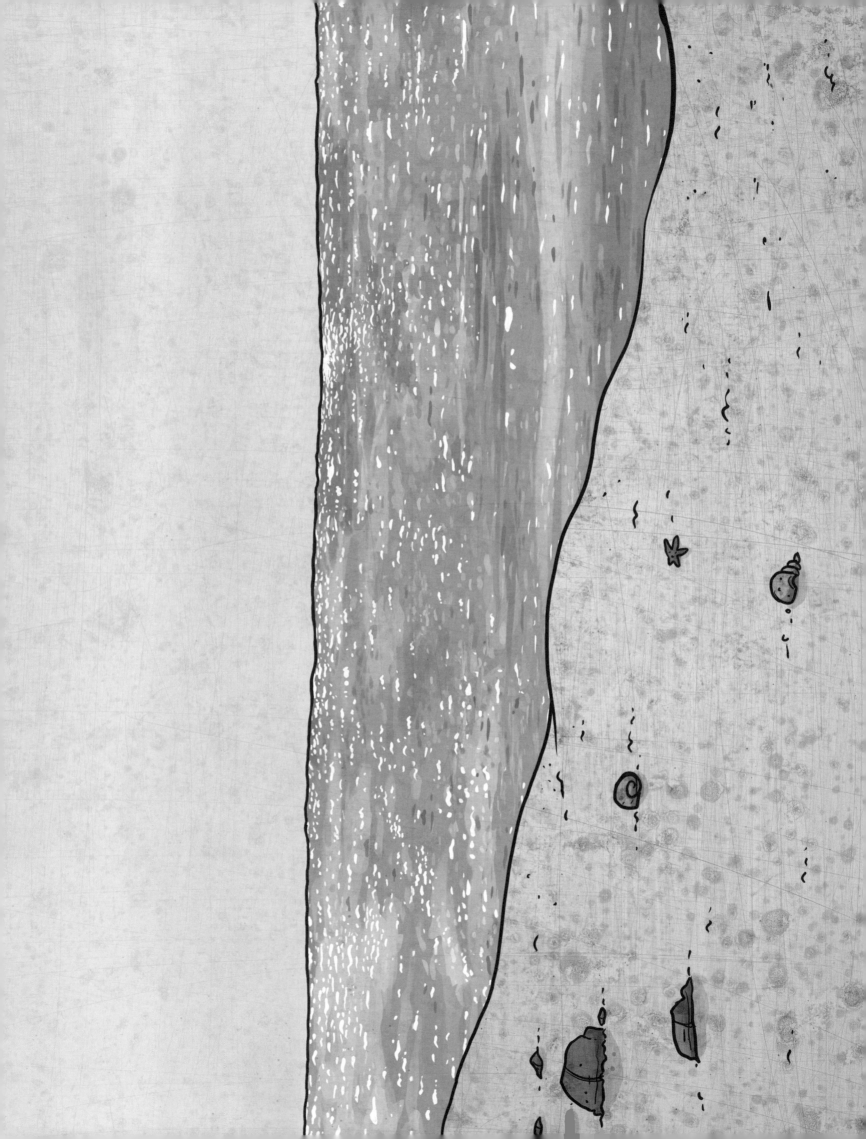